DISNEY's TREASURE PLANET

SPACE CASE

Written by Kim Yaged

Illustrated by Denise Shimabukuro,
Marco Ghiglione, and the Disney Storybook Artists

Designed by Disney's Global Design Group

Random House 🏠 New York
A Random House PICTUREBACK® Book

Library of Congress Control Number: 2002100657

ISBN: 0-7364-2017-7

www.randomhouse.com/kids/disney

Printed in the United States of America

10 9 8 7 6 5 4 3 2 1

Oh! Hi! Hey there! My name is B.E.N. That's short for Bio-Electronic Navigator. The navigator's in charge of leading a crew on its adventures through outer space, exploring new and exciting galaxies—places like the Lagoon Nebula, Proteus One, the Planet Pelsinor . . . Okay, so maybe the captain helps a little, too, but I am a *very* important robot!

And this is my story. It's all about the adventures I had on a mysterious place called Treasure Planet. We're talking pirates, treasure, a missing memory circuit (that would be mine), a treasure map, and my best buddy, Jimmy, the greatest solar surfer who ever lived.

Way before I met Jimmy, there was this scary pirate named Captain Flint. Captain Flint's idea of a good time was stealing and, well . . . more stealing! That guy stole a lot. And when I say a lot, I mean *a lot*—gold, silver, gems, you name it! Anything Captain Flint could get his hands on he would take. He even stole *me*!

And once he had me, Captain Flint wouldn't go anywhere without me. I guess that's because I was his navigator. But this guy took it a little too far. I had to taste his food before he would eat it. I stood guard outside the bathroom door when he took bubble baths. He even made me sleep in his cabin—not that I got much sleep. Boy, could that guy snore!

Those were the good old days! Well, come to think of it, they were pretty, uh, well—boring. That is, until we stumbled onto Treasure Planet. A group of way smart alien scientists built it a long time ago. Captain Flint discovered these magical portals and figured out how to transport himself anywhere in the galaxy! So he stole and stole and stole some more! And he hid all his loot deep inside Treasure Planet.

Oh, yeah, we're talking big-time cash here. But Flint soon got so greedy that even his crew left him. And before he died, he pulled out my memory circuit so I couldn't tell anyone about his precious treasure.

That's when things really got weird! If you think I ramble now, well, you should have seen me then! You have no idea what it's like to have your memory circuit pulled out. Come to think of it, maybe I don't, either—I can't remember!

So there I was, stuck in the caves in the center of Treasure Planet with no memory circuit. I started to wander around, trying to find a way out. Without my memory circuit, this was no walk in the park. I ended up going around in circles. Finally, I made it to the surface of Treasure Planet. I'd tell you how I did it, but I CAN'T REMEMBER!

Treasure Planet was really something! Can you say *plants*?
Cagefungus, centipede trees, trumpet plants—we're talking
green as far as the eye could see! And it was hot! Robots may
not perspire, but we leak oil like you've never seen! Trust me,
it wasn't pretty.

Without Captain Flint, there was no one to do my monthly repairs. I had to talk the lunar eels into charging my eye sockets and the astral birds into buffing my metal. I'm telling you, a robot's life is very tiring. Constant maintenance!

Getting neat and pretty always made me hungry, so I'd make myself a meal of my favorite Treasure Planet snacks— exploding astro nuts, snarling bite-back bananas, and flying pop rockets. Not your idea of a family picnic? Not mine either! But I got used to it. Although, I have to admit, sometimes I was just too tired to chase after those pop rockets.

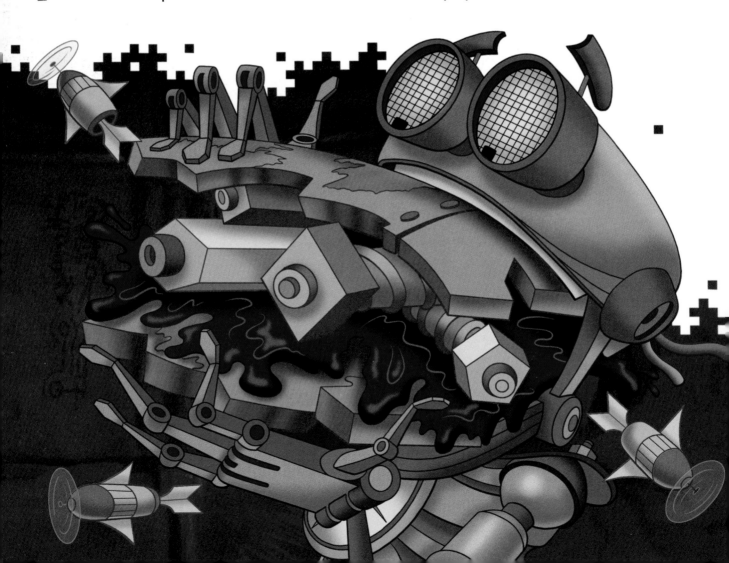

In my spare time—which was most of the time—I invented games. Galaxy checkers, spacer checkers, gravity checkers, solar checkers—let me tell you, I had checkers covered! Until I discovered you need two to play! And, may I remind you, I was all alone!

But with no one else around, I was in charge. I called myself Captain B.E.N. and I had to obey my every command!

It wasn't such a bad life, but I have to admit it got lonely. Which is why I was happier than a lunar eel during an Arcturian meteor shower when Jimmy and his friends showed up. Finally, someone to play checkers with! There were Jimmy, Morph, Dr. Doppler, and Captain Amelia. Then all these pirates showed up—and the fun really started!

You see, the pirates were after Jimmy and his friends. They were in trouble and really needed my help. So I rescued Jimmy and his crew, risked my life to get the treasure map back—knocking out a few laser cannons along the way— and led them to the treasure. I think it's safe to say some of us might not be here today if it weren't for me and my fearless heroics.

All right, all right, here's the *real* story. I did help out, but my pal Jimmy was the one who truly saved the day. Like I said, there was this map. Only, it was a special kind of map, and Jimmy was the only one who knew how to work it, which was really important because it opened the portal that led to the treasure.

So after Jimmy found the treasure—this is the really amazing part—he found my memory circuit, too! Rainbows and fireworks and a three-scoop sundae with purps on top— that's what it was like when Jimmy put my memory circuit back in.

But there wasn't any time to celebrate because I suddenly remembered that Captain Flint had left a booby trap to protect the treasure. We had only two minutes and thirty-four seconds to get off the planet before it was blown to smithereenies!

Jimmy led us back to the ship so we could skedaddle, but its thrusters were damaged by flying space trash. My hero Jimmy never gave up. He swooped through the skies on a solar surfer back toward the portal— risking his life so that our ship could escape before Treasure Planet exploded. I've never seen anything quite like it!

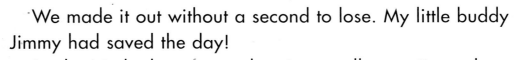

We made it out without a second to lose. My little buddy Jimmy had saved the day!

But here's the best part: when it was all over, Jimmy let me give him a hug of thanks.

And even better than that, he hugged me back!